Trailokya Nath Mukharji

# Monograph

of the brass and copper manufactures of Bengal

Trailokya Nath Mukharji

**Monograph**
*of the brass and copper manufactures of Bengal*

ISBN/EAN: 9783337387013

Printed in Europe, USA, Canada, Australia, Japan

Cover: Foto ©Andreas Hilbeck / pixelio.de

More available books at **www.hansebooks.com**

# MONOGRAPH

ON THE

# BRASS AND COPPER MANUFACTURES OF BENGAL.

. BY

TRAILOKYA NATH MUKHARJI, F.L.S.,

INDIAN MUSEUM, CALCUTTA.

CALCUTTA:

OFFICE OF THE SUPERINTENDENT, GOVERNMENT PRINTING, INDIA.

1894

CALCUTTA :

GOVERNMENT OF INDIA CENTRAL PRINTING OFFICE,

8, HASTINGS STREET.

# Brass, Bronze, and Copper Manufactures of Bengal.*

**The ancient and the modern.**—In India the most primitive and the most modern things exist side by side. The wild aborigine of the jungle is the next-door neighbour of the man of highest modern culture. Primitive usages and appliances have also survived the changes of thousands of years and maintain a hoary existence side by side with the less romantic customs and things of modern times. The fire-drill is still made to yield the fire required for sacrificial purposes, while on the same spot the lucifer match is struck to light the fragrant havanna. The ancient bullock-chariot creeps beside the railway with its snorting locomotive and rushing train, and under the roadside telegraph wire the slow messenger goes his weary way carrying letters written on palm-leaf by means of an iron style. The hands of the sturdy maid bend beneath the weight of massive brass-wristlets of the most primitive make, while the arms of her delicate mistress glitter with facetted gold-bangles of the most refined workmanship. Thus, in innumerable instances, the most ancient are seen to live side by side with the most modern customs and usages. Native India bears the silent impress of man's social and domestic history from the earliest of ages, though it possesses hardly any authentic record of kings and battles, invasions and massacres.

**Development of Metal Manufactures.**—These living relics of the past invite a minute research to trace step by step the gradual development of the metal manufactures of India. The dried-up shells of wild gourds which hung handy from trees of the primitive forests no doubt formed the first drinking-cup of the earliest man in India. Those shells are still used as such by religious itinerants whose austere life permits only the simple habits of prehistoric ages, but no luxurious innovations of later days. But when the art of copying vegetable and animal objects in stone was learnt, when gold and copper were discovered and the manufacture of brass invented, the householders began to make, though not without a protest against the change, vessels and other articles of stone or metal similar in shape to that of the natural objects employed in domestic use, chase, war, or personal adornment. In brass the gourd shell gradually developed into the *Lota* and the *Ghati*, and in copper the scooped-out rhinoceros-horn, which on account of its comparative rarity and durability must have been a very valuable utensil in ancient times, and the oblations poured out of which are still considered highly acceptable to gods and ancestral manes, became the sacrificial vessel called *Koshá* of modern days. The large round leaf of the lotus, or the copy of it made by pinning together smaller leaves of other plants, which, together with the plantain leaf, is still used as a plate all over the country, is the original of the modern *Thálá*, and one half of the round *Bel* rind or the cocoa-nut shell, still used as a cup, spoon, or ladle, gave the model for the modern *Báti* or the *Katorá*. Hollowed pieces of wood, still used, specially in jungle tracts, to keep water, milk, or pea-soup during feasts and festivals, formed models for large brass jars called *Ghará*, or for circular basins called *Gámlá*. The iron arrow-head of later times was the copy of the pointed deer-horn sharpened by rubbing it on stones, and the modern plough that of the

---

* Brass, vernacular *Pittal* or *Pital*, is an alloy of copper and zinc; bro nae, called also bell-metal, vernacular *Kánsi*, is an alloy of copper and tin; *Bharan*, an alloy of copper, zinc and tin, generally sold as *Kánsi*; copper, vernacular *Támra* or *Támá*.

forked branch of a tree used to scratch the soil in primitive agriculture. Similarly, flowers and leaves of trees, such as the *Champá*, the cocoa-nut and the *Pán*, gave form to various brass ornaments of personal adornment. As a sign of increasing prosperity of the people, household utensils, hitherto made of basket-work or clay, are now being made of brass, as more suitable for domestic purposes on account of their portability, durability, and greater purity. The rice-washer made of shining brass now glitters in every utensil shop, though that made of sliced bamboo by the low-caste *Dom* is still almost in universal use. The vessel called *Hándi*, used to boil rice, is being made of brass, though that made of clay is still used by high and low, as the former is costly, requires daily cleaning and scrubbing, and *is* said to make the food cooked in it heating and harmful. The incense-holder called *Dhunachi*, may now be had of brass, though fifty years ago solely that made of clay burnt the *Dhup* and *Dhuná* of the Hindus and the *Lobán* of the Muhammadans. Thus, within recent years, things formerly made of wood, bamboo, or clay, are, when found feasible, being made of brass or copper.

**Purity measured by antiquity.**—Reluctance for change, which is always present in man's nature in every age and clime, and also his vain efforts to withstand its irresistibility, are nowhere better displayed than in the measurement of the purity of a thing in proportion to its antiquity. This standard, according to which things obtained a higher or a lower place on the platform of religion or caste, is not confined to discoveries or inventions alone, nor to implements or utensils, nor to wood, stone, or metals, but also extends to every walk of life, from the obsolete thoughts and practices of old times to articles of food or raiment introduced into the country in later ages. If no other consideration comes into play, the greater purity of a thing is but expressive of its greater antiquity. The newer the thing, the lesser is it acceptable to gods and men in a religious and caste point of view. The greater purity of the cane-sugar than date-sugar, and of the pulse *Mung* than *Másh* (Phaserlus sp.) betrays the earlier introduction of the former and the later introduction of the latter. Potato and cabbage, brought almost within the memory of man, have not yet quite got over the stigma of their foreign origin; while the pine and the custard apple have become acceptable to gods and men, all trace of their early history having been lost in the dim haze of four centuries of Indian life. Similarly, wool is purer than cotton, but silk, which no doubt is a later introduction, has evidently been credited with the virtues of wool, being an allied product, and being too valuable and too powerful an article to submit to be relegated among impure things, though its production entails the sacrifice of myriads of lives. Following this standard of measuring the antiquity of a thing by its greater or lesser purity in the eye of religion and caste, we find here a corroboration of the results attained by anthropological researches in other parts of the world, which have given a clue to the early progress of man from the use of wood, bone, horn, and stone, to that of gold, copper, bronze, and iron. Gold being found in the native state no doubt was the first metal to draw the attention of man, and it therefore rightly received the name *Ayas*, or that which attracts, which name was subsequently transferred to iron, owing probably to its magnetic properties. Gold, however, is too rare a metal to come into extensive use, except, as the sacred books assert, in the Age of Truth, when the world was sinless, and when the people necessarily could afford to eat off golden plates and drink out of golden cups. In point of purity, and consequently in point of antiquity, copper comes next, which, though in India scarcely found in the native state, was easily smelted from its ore by spontaneous jungle fires that no doubt raged in the primitive forests as they rage now in spite of trained rangers and watchful guards. The use of copper revolutionised the habits and customs of the age, and from the day of its discovery a new era may be said to have dawned upon the early history of man.

**Antiquity and purity of metals.**—It is very probable that at first all household articles were made of pure copper, but in time it partly gave way to its more gold-like alloy, brass, and later on to bronze. Copper being first in the field is held to be the purest of all inferior metals; brass coming next, occupies the second place; and bronze, though more costly, beautiful and useful, and less harmful owing to its greater resisting power against rust and corrosion, is the last in point of purity, and is liable to defilement by the touch of men not approved by caste. In Europe the use of bronze—i.e., the alloy of copper and tin—might have preceded that of brass, the alloy of copper and zinc; but in India it seems to have been the reverse—at least the relation between purity and antiquity seems so to indicate. This is explained by the almost total absence of workable tin ores in India, though zinc is also very scarce. The same forest-fires which discovered for man the existence of copper by smelting the ores, must also have taught him the preparation of brass by melting into an alloy zinc-blendes associated with copper, which sparsely occurred in the neighbourhood of tracts where the Aryans formed their first settlements.

**Supersession of copper.**—Though brass came into extensive use in the manufacture of household utensils, copper was not altogether discarded. As observed before, things in India somehow or other get mixed up with religion. From birth to death, from the building of a house to the wearing of a shell-bracelet, all form occasions for a series of thanksgiving and devotion of man to the service of God. The most ancient things having the longest standing and the closest alliance with religion, the latter becomes their last refuge, when discoveries, inventions, and innovations have driven them from every other field, from every nook and corner of Hindu household and Hindu social life. Old things, therefore, die hard in India, and do not die at all if they have fairly associated themselves with religious ceremonials. From the most primitive gourd-shell to the costliest of plates, each gets a place allotted to itself, and modestly goes on performing its duties and functions for all time to come. Pure copper, all but discarded from every other household use, has nevertheless retained its place in religion, and is now chiefly employed in the manufacture of sacrificial vessels, at least so far as Bengal is concerned. Since the advent of the Muhammadans, however, who use it tinned, copper is also largely employed in the manufacture of ordinary utensils for Musalman households. Brass, being less liable to defilement than bronze, is employed for making articles which can be allowed to be used, scrubbed, and cleaned by people of all castes, and being also cheaper, is largely utilised in the manufacture of articles of common and constant use, chiefly water-vessels and cooking-pots. Bronze, less liable to be tarnished and affected by acids and salts, and at the same time being more costly, is reserved for dishes, plates, cups, and drinking vessels.

**Metal-working castes.**—It appears that in the Hindu social system there were originally no separate castes to work the different metals. Vaisyas and the higher Sudras, under the general name of " Karmokárs " or " artisans,

might freely choose any metal to work it as a profession, until it became hereditary, and gradually differentiated and stereotyped itself into a separate caste-
occupation. Thus, jewellers and workers in gold and silver became the Swarnakár
caste, and braziers and workers in copper became the Kánsári caste of our days,
while the name Karmokár is now exclusively applied to the caste which works
in iron and steel. Three classes of metal workers—one working in gold and silver,
the second in brass and copper, and the third in iron and steel - thus differentiated
themselves into three separate castes, with the invariable injunction against inter-
eating and inter-marrying. They were, however, all held highly respectable, in
a caste point of view, until the degradation of the gold and silver smiths, the
Swarnakárs, which tradition ascribes to their incorrigible propensity to inter-
fere with the precious metals entrusted to their care for the manufacture
of plates or ornaments. But even before the advent of Western education
in Bengal, which in various directions has upset the old caste-professions,
the privilege of working any of the metals never remained the exclusive
property of any one caste. Thus, many of the Karmokárs of Dacca have
long forgotten their caste-profession of manipulating steel and iron, and
have acquired a wide fame for their workmanship in gold and silver; and
the Kánsáris of Bhawánipur, near Calcutta, have for some time past taken
to the manufacture of gold ornaments, silver plates, and delicate instruments, in preference to making copper pots, brass goglets, and bronze
plates. On the other hand, all castes without distinction seem to have
trespassed into the hereditary profession of the braziers themselves, and are
seen busy hammering copper, moulding brass, and polishing bronze, or
selling the utensils as wholesale merchants, retail shopkeepers, or wandering
hawkers. In the hilly districts of Western Bengal, metal-artisans, or at
least certain sections of them, seem to have gradually evolved out of the
aboriginal or semi-aboriginal iron-smelters. As they became Hinduised and
improved their professional position by advancing from iron-smelting to iron-
working, and from iron-working to working in more valuable metals, they, on
the authority of one of the later sacred books, traced their descent from a
Hindu divinity and laid claim to the same respectability as is enjoyed by their
brother-craftsmen in other parts of the country. On one of those occasions,
which were so very common in the infancy of the world, a mighty demon rose
into power and drove away the minor deities from their celestial possessions. The
god Siva, by virtue of whose reckless boon the demon had acquired such in-
vincibility, was besought to save the hapless celestials from this terrible cala-
mity. Taking pity upon the fugitive gods, Siva created a man to fight the
demon, and sent him down to earth fully equipped with blacksmiths' tools.
Meeting the demon, the man challenged him to a single combat, but he laughed
at his presumption, considering that so tiny a creature would scarcely form a
mouthful to eat. The man then defied him to enter his furnace, which request,
with the customary stupidity of a giant, he readily complied with. The man
began to blow his bellows hard, but the giant inside the furnace, with the stub-
bornness of his race, would neither stir, nor cry, nor scream, though his body soon
got red-hot, melted, and began to flow out in all directions in the form of
molten masses of iron, copper, and other metals. This was the origin of the
metals, and that man was the ancestor of the artisans who work in metals.
They were subdivided into eight classes according to the metal in which
they worked or things they made :—(1) Lohár-kámár who work in iron ;

(2) Pitule-kámár who work in brass; (3) Kánsári-kámár who work in bronze; (4) Swarna-kámár, who work in gold; (5) Ghatrá-kámár, who make imitation fruits in iron, figures of owls, the vehicle of the goddess of wealth, and who use the charcoal left behind of wood with which dead-bodies have been cremated; (6) Chánd-kámár, who make brass mirrors; (7) Dhokrá-kámár; and (8) Támra-kámár, who work in iron and copper. But the Kánsáris of Central Bengal hold a more recognised position in the Hindu social system. Various stories are related about the origin of this caste in the sacred Puránas, specially in the Brahmavaivartta and the Brihaddharma Puránas, but they do not deserve to be mentioned here. Suffice it to say that the Kánsáris themselves claim to be Vaisyas and one of the five sections of the great commercial class of Bengal. These five sections are:—(1) Gandha-banik, or the scent and spice sellers; (2) Sankha-banik, or conch-shell sellers; (3) Kansa-banik, or sellers of brass and bronze utensils; (4) Mani-banik, or sellers of precious stones; and (5) Suvarna-banik, or sellers of gold and silver. The general public, however, consider the first four as higher Sudras for whom a good Bráhman can officiate as a priest. The last, or the Suvarna-baniks, have suffered in public estimation owing to a royal edict, about the cause of which there are many stories current. The most current story is to the effect that more than eight hundred years ago a king of Bengal caused a number of golden calves to be made and distributed among the Bráhmans. One of these being filled with liquid lac-dye was taken to a Suvarna-banik for sale. In order to examine the quality of the gold, he cut into the calf and thereby let out the blood-like liquid. The inexpiable guilt of killing a cow was thus fastened upon him, and the king, who had a grudge against the caste, at once degraded it to the position of the lower Sudras. In Behar the brazier caste is called the Kasera, who work in copper, prepare brass and bronze, and mould and beat them into utensils. Another caste, called the Thatará, also work in metals, whose speciality lies in polishing and engraving the utensils made by the Kasera and manufacturing ornaments.

**People engaged in manufacture and trade.**—The following table shows the total population, the number of persons belonging to the three recognised brazier castes, and the number of people actually engaged in manufacturing and selling brass and copper ware in each Division of Bengal :—

| Name of Division. | Total population. | Total number of Kánsáris. | Total number of Kaseras. | Total number of Thatáras. | Number of people actually engaged in brass and bronze. |
|---|---|---|---|---|---|
| Burdwan | 7,888,818 | 5,377 | ... | 825 | 25,454 |
| Presidency | 8,533,126 | 9,362 | ... | 161 | 13,333 |
| Rajshahi | 8,019,187 | 1,005 | ... | 43 | 5,345 |
| Dacca | 9,844,127 | 1,209 | ... | ... | 11,167 |
| Chittagong | 4,190,061 | 294 | ... | ... | 1,902 |
| Patna | 15,811,014 | ... | 14,256 | 13,245 | 22,545 |
| Bhagalpur | 8,582,490 | 3,121 | ... | 10,007 | 10,611 |
| Orissa | 4,047,353 | 13,979 | ... | 4,436 | 20,776 |
| Chutia Nagpur | 4,628,792 | 3,158 | ... | 3,061 | 7,550 |
| Total Bengal | 71,346,967 | 36,604 | 14,256 | 39,277 | 119,064 |

The details of the last column in the preceding table—*viz.*, the number of people actually engaged in the manufacture and sale of brass and copper ware—are given in the following statement:—

| NAME OF DIVISION. | Brass workers and sellers. | Brass pot makers and sellers. | Copper workers and sellers. | Brass and copper wire drawers and sellers. | Bronze workers and sellers. | General workers in brass, copper, and bronze. | Brass and copper dealers. |
|---|---|---|---|---|---|---|---|
| Burdwan . . . | 6,153 | 11,971 | 111 | 1 | 3,724 | 3,979 | 515 |
| Presidency . . . | 1,396 | 5,101 | 90 | 714 | 3,473 | 1,861 | 758 |
| Rajshahi . . . | 462 | 2,227 | 41 | ... | 945 | 504 | 167 |
| Dacca . . . | 2,220 | 2,320 | 109 | ... | 2,073 | 1,421 | 3,234 |
| Chittagong . . . | 406 | 349 | 71 | ... | 128 | 353 | 596 |
| Patna . . . | 3,422 | 2,267 | 23 | 74 | 7,753 | 0,264 | 22 |
| Bhagalpur . . . | 1,683 | 2,239 | 13 | ... | 1,226 | 4,924 | 436 |
| Orissa . . . | 5,279 | 1,503 | ... | ... | 12,616 | 239 | 1,149 |
| Chutia Nagpur . . | 2,015 | 813 | ... | ... | 1,317 | 3,446 | 59 |
| TOTAL . | 22,035 | 29,700 | 398 | 789 | 34,255 | 25,961 | 5,926 |

**Raw Materials : Copper.**—No indigenous copper is now available, the smelting of the metal in this country having almost entirely ceased. The imported metal is now solely employed for the manufacture of copper vessels. Only sheet copper is used for such purposes. Old copper collected in the country and imported copper bricks and tiles are melted down and made into brass and bronze, but are not used directly in the manufacture of copper vessels. Copper vessels, however, are never made by casting into moulds, for the manufacturers do not know how to melt this metal, without the addition of zinc, tin or lead. That known as the Russian copper is preferred for the manufacture of copper vessels. The following table shows the import of copper into Bengal during the five years ending 1892-93 :—

| | 1888-89. | | 1889-90. | | 1890-91. | | 1891-92. | | 1892-93. | |
|---|---|---|---|---|---|---|---|---|---|---|
| | Cwt. | R | Cwt. | R | Cwt. | R | Cwt. | R | Cwt. | R |
| Old copper . . | 151 | 4,921 | 100 | 2,600 | 79 | 2,125 | 884 | 11,096 | 1,169 | 32,972 |
| Unwrought: Tiles, ingots, cakes and bricks . . | 9,396 | 1,86,199 | 87,834 | 21,96,961 | 51,320 | 20,69,353 | 58,082 | 22,07,251 | 9,285 | 3,80,281 |
| Unwrought: Other sorts . . . | 22,511 | 12,94,090 | 79,910 | 26,68,456 | 51,116 | 20,32,064 | 89,877 | 31,59,290 | 49,510 | 16,32,767 |
| Wrought: Lametta | 1,019 | 2,41,382 | 991 | 2,95,937 | 1,769 | 3,67,086 | 1,350 | 2,91,086 | 1,489 | 3,01,585 |
| „ Mixed . | 23,967 | 12,57,137 | 41,463 | 16,04,588 | 26,047 | 13,65,441 | 35,263 | 14,18,909 | 33,963 | 15,12,653 |
| „ Sheets, etc. . | 2,388 | 1,53,817 | 24,782 | 10,35,635 | 16,585 | 7,39,540 | 17,364 | 8,06,273 | 17,364 | 7,90,601 |
| TOTAL . | 54,272 | 31,42,546 | 234,820 | 59,27,177 | 146,946 | 65,75,809 | 196,792 | 78,97,607 | 110,790 | 46,40,982 |

**Brass.**—Brass is still made in this country, but its manufacture has somewhat suffered of late years owing to the import of sheet-brass from foreign countries. The following table shows the import of brass into Bengal during the five years ending 1892-93 :—

| Brass. | 1888-89. | | 1889-90. | | 1890-91. | | 1891-92. | | 1892-93. | |
|---|---|---|---|---|---|---|---|---|---|---|
| | Cwt. | R | Cwt. | R | Cwt. | R | Cwt. | R | Cwt. | R |
| Wrought (including sheet-brass) | 2,915 | 1,52,080 | 2,996 | 1,70,392 | 2,963 | 1,61,433 | 2,593 | 1,38,157 | 2,102 | 1,10,438 |

Imported sheet-brass is only used in the manufacture of hammered utensils, and country brass both for hammered and cast vessels. Brass is still made in many places. Generally country brass is an alloy consisting of 2℔ of copper and 1¼℔ of zinc, but that with 1¼℔ of zinc to the same quantity of copper is considered a better quality, and still better that with copper and zinc in the proportion of two to one. But brass of such superior quality is now seldom made, except by special order. Inferior brass is also made of 3 parts of copper, 2 of zinc and 1 of lead. A very small quantity of lead is often added to brass in order to make it soft and malleable. Copper sells at R46 per cwt., zinc at R9, and brass at R42. It is, therefore, advantageous to the maker of brass to add as much zinc to the alloy as he can possibly do. Brass is made in the following way :—A round hole, 2 feet in diameter and 3 feet deep, is dug on the floor of the shop, upon which an iron grate is placed. This iron grate is covered by a thin coating of clay, leaving several small openings at intervals. The hole is then enclosed by a circular clay wall, 3 feet high, open at the top. Immediately outside the wall a small aperture is made on the floor leading to the hole under the iron grate. This is the furnace, which is technically known as the *sdl*. The object of the small openings left on the iron grate is to allow the ashes of the fuel to fall through them into the hole beneath, as well as to allow a free circulation of air. The aperture made on the floor connecting it with the hole underneath the grate ensures the free passage of the air, as well as allows the ashes to be taken out when the hole is filled with them. Crucibles, called *muchi*, of various sizes, made of clay, mixed with sand, rice-husk, and chopped jute, are kept ready beforehand. These are filled with copper and zinc pieces, in the proportion mentioned above, into which a handful of salt is put to serve as a flux. Borax is sometimes substituted for salt, especially when some hard old brass has to be melted down. The crucibles are next arranged in the furnace and covered with the fuel, which in the neighbourhood of Calcutta is generally coke, but in other places charcoal. The fire is then lit, and it takes three hours to melt the metals and to form them into an alloy. Formerly bellows were worked to supply a blast to the fire, but the present construction of the furnace has rendered it unnecessary, the air passing through the aperture on the floor to the bottom of the furnace, and thence to the fuel through the small openings in the grate, having been found quite sufficient for the purpose. Country brass is either hammered into utensils or immediately cast into moulds, the process of which will be described hereafter.

**Bronze or Bell-metal** (*Kánsá*).—Bronze is not imported, but made in the country. It is an alloy consisting of seven parts of copper and two parts of tin. There is a saying current among the braziers—

> Sátáy doráy kore jaro
> Téte áno táte garo.
> Mix seven of copper with two of tin,
> Heat it alternately and beat it thin.

Bronze is made within a furnace either in the same way as brass or the fusion of the metals is effected in a small open hole, in which the copper is first placed and covered with the fuel. The blast is supplied through a bent tube connected with the bellows. When the copper is sufficiently heated, the tin is placed upon it. Both the metals now melt, mix and form bronze. This kind of bronze is good for gongs. Bronze when made is either at once cast into moulds of vessels or set apart to be worked afterwards. Pure bronze, as a rule, is only employed in the manufacture of plates and other articles that require to be made by hammering. For cast articles an impure alloy called *Bharan* or *Toul* is chiefly used. This is generally made by adding some brass or zinc into pure bronze, or some tin into brass. There is no fixed proportion of the metals employed to produce *Bharan*, but the greater the quantity of zinc in the alloy, the more is it of inferior quality. *Bharan*, in short, is brass with a little admixture of tin to give it a whitish appearance and to enable the dealers to sell it as *Kánsá* to the public. A kind of bronze, called gun-metal, is made in some places with one part of tin to ten of copper. A small quantity of lead is also sometimes added to *Bharan* to make it soft and easily workable. In some places of Behar the following bronze alloys are prepared :—(1) *Kánsá*, lead and brass mixed; (2) *Bharat*, brass and copper mixed ; (3) *Phulkánsá*, pewter, copper, and silver mixed. Tin sells at R70, and *Bharan* and bronze from R50 to R80 per cwt.

**Mode of Manufacture—Hammered Articles.**—Utensils are either hammered into shape from sheet-brass or sheet-copper, or from country brass or cast into moulds, or partly cast and partly beaten. Sheet-brass (except scraps) or sheet-copper are never melted and made into cast articles, but are always beaten into shape and joined if an article is made of several pieces. All cast articles are made from brass or bronze prepared in the country. Copper articles are always beaten, never moulded. If a plate or any other article consisting of one or more pieces of the metal is required to be made, the copper or the brass sheet is first marked out by a pair of compasses and the piece or pieces cut off by a kind of scissors called *kátari*. It is then made into the required shape by alternate heating and hammering, and finally turned in the lathe. Some of the larger vessels, specially water and cooking pots, are made of two, three, or more pieces. Each piece is first reduced to shape by continual hammering and afterwards joined together by means of borax and a solder, which is a kind of hard brass, being an alloy of copper and zinc. The final polish is given in the lathe. Beaten bronze articles require more frequent heating in the fire and hammering as it is brittle, and readily breaks under the hammer. Bronze articles require to be tempered by dipping them in water while red hot. Hindus of Bengal do not use copper vessels for ordinary household purposes, but only as sacrificial utensils. Muhammadans put them to domestic use, but get them tinned when they can afford to do so. Buyers prefer hammered to cast articles, as the former can only be made of superior qualities of brass and bronze. In point of fact most of the cast articles sold as bronze are not made of bronze or *Kánsá* but *Bharan*. The workmen of Kharár in the Midnapur District can only beat out vessels of inferior bronze. Bronze or *Kánsá* vessels are never made by joining two or more pieces together, as there is strong superstition against this practice.

**Cast utensils.**—For cast articles a mould is first prepared which is called *chhánch*. The mould is made of very fine clay mixed with chopped jute. The worker, taking a lump of soft clay in his hand, presses and flattens it with his thumbs on the inner surface of the vessel of which a copy is to be made. Sometimes a wooden or a clay mould of the vessel to be cast is first made and on which the clay is pressed, or in some places, as at Ránaghát, a wax *fac-simile* is used for the purpose, the wax being subsequently melted out. When the whole inner surface of the vessel is in this way covered with a layer of clay, one or more incisions are made upon it to allow the clay-coating to be separated in pieces from the vessel when dry. These pieces are subsequently joined together and the mouth closed, rendering it a hollow clay vessel of exactly the same shape as the metal vessel to be cast. It thus becomes the core of the mould. When this core is thoroughly dry, a similar layer of clay is put upon it, and the required number of incisions made. This outer layer of clay is separated from the core when dry, and is found to have formed a cavity all round between it and the core by drying and shrinking. This cavity is generally of the same breadth as the required thickness of the vessel to be cast. If it is not so, then the worker has to scrape off a portion of the clay from its inner surface in order to produce the required vacuum between the outer shell of clay and the inner core. This done, the outer shell is again put upon the core, the incisions joined, and the mouth closed, leaving only a small aperture for the molten metal to pass into the cavity between the outer layer of clay and the inner core. Very often a layer of clay is put first on the outside and then another on the inside of the vessel. These layers of clay are separated and joined together by which the required cavity is necessarily formed between them. The mould thus completed is next thoroughly dried. It is then put upside down upon the crucible, which has previously been filled with pieces of the metals of which the alloy—either brass, bronze, or *Bharan*—is to be prepared in the furnace. The crucibles are therefore of different sizes, according to the size of the vessel to be made and the required quantity of the alloy to be formed. They are capable of holding from $\frac{1}{4}$lb to 20lb of the alloy. After fitting the mould to the crucible they are joined together by a thick plaster of clay, so that both the crucible and the mould look like one lump of clay. They are then arranged in the furnace. Four or more crucibles and moulds can go into the furnace at a time, according to the size of the vessels to be made and the space they would occupy. When the worker perceives, which he does by experience, that the metals have thoroughly melted inside the crucible and have formed the alloy, he brings each crucible and mould out of the furnace by iron tongs, called *Sánrái*, and turns it upside down. The crucible is now turned over the mould, and the molten metal enters the cavity in it by the aperture left in the mouth. Before taking the crucible out of the furnace it is very important to see that the mould has also become thoroughly "ripo," *i.e.*, of the same temperature as the molten metals, as otherwise it would burst. Considerable experience in the work is necessary in order to be able to guess that both the metal and the mould are ready to be taken out of the furnace. If the moulds are not joined to the crucibles, they have to be made red hot somewhere outside the furnace before the molten metal is poured into them. When sufficiently cool, the crucible and the mould are broken to pieces and the cast vessel taken out. The combined weight of the copper and the other metal placed in the crucible slightly exceeds the weight of the vessel to be made. This is necessary, so that the metal may reach the remotest parts of the cavity in the mould, specially the bottom, and no vacuum left. This excess quantity of the metal forms a small projection outside the aperture of the mould. This is now broken off from the vessel by an iron rod, called the *Sábal*, as well as other projections that may have formed on other sides. Smaller irregularities are next chiselled or filed off. The vessel is then glued to the lathe by means of a compound made of lac, sál (*Shorea robusta*), resin, and brick-dust, and all remaining irregularities and unevenness are polished off by turning and planing upon this instrument. While still turning upon the lathe, the final polish is given by pressing upon it a small ball of hair steeped in sweet-oil. Some vessels, such as cooking-pots, called *Boknos*, require to be put into shape by much hammering after a preliminary cast has been made. Larger vessels, such as the water-pots called *Ghárás*, are made by joining two or three pieces together which are separately cast. The price of a vessel, specially that of eating and drinking utensils, depends, not so much upon the superior quality of the metal, as upon the polish given to it while on the lathe. The same class of vessel which would sell at twelve annas per lb would fetch R2 per lb if highly polished. The wide celebrity which the bronze plates, cups, tumblers, and other articles made at Khánkrá, near Murshidabad, have acquired, is no doubt due to the purity of the metal employed in their manufacture, but to a still greater degree they owe their reputation to the high polish given to them.

Instruments.—The instruments used in the manufacture of copper and brass vessels are simple and few in number. They may be named as follows:—The hammer and the anvil, which are of various shapes and sizes, the chisel, the iron tongs, the file, the lathe, the scraper used for the lathe called *Noyáli*, a rod of iron called *Sábal* of various sizes, a small piece of triangular iron to scrape the clay mould, called *Chhvri*, or knife, scissors called *Kátari*, wooden hammers, bellows, two-legged wood, called *Dothengo* for holding *Sábals* etc., etc.

System of Manufacture and Prices.—Copper, brass, and bronze articles are generally made by the braziers to order given to them by dealers or capitalists, who supply the raw materials or advance money for their purchase. The makers are paid by weight of articles turned out, the rate being R20 to R50 per cwt. of bronze utensils and R15 to R40 of brass and copper. Labour being cheap in the interior of the districts of Burdwan, Bankura, and Midnapur, large quantities of vessels sold in Calcutta are made there. The utensils are also sold retail by weight, the price being 8 annas per lb of copper, 6 to 8 annas of brass, and 12 annas to R2 of bronze.

Patterns.—Patterns are distinguished by the shapes of the vessels, not by different styles of ornamentation, for except in a few sacrificial vessels and water-pots no decoration is employed. Indeed, decoration in articles for daily use will be useless, for it cannot last long under the wear and tear of daily scrubbing and cleaning. Patterns as distinguished by shapes generally take their names from those of the places where they were first made, such as the *Bálescori* from Balasore, *Gayeswari* from Gayá, *Khánkrái* from Khánkrá, etc. New patterns are also sometimes introduced in commemoration of some notable event, such as the *Elokeshi-báti*, after a woman named Elokeshi, who some years ago was murdered by her husband for misconduct with the monk in charge of the shrine at Tárakeswar in the Hooghly District. The event created considerable stir at the time, owing to the fact that a holy man was implicated in it, and that the woman was most vilely misguided by the machinations of her step-mother. The horror for the sin committed by the monk and the sympathy of the people for the injured husband found vent, among other things, in the introduction of various household articles of new patterns bearing the name of the woman, such as fish-knives (with which the woman was hacked), *Sáris*, utensils, etc. Other patterns receive their names from the fact of their being ribbed or not ribbed, polished or not polished, etc., etc.

**Classification of Articles.**—Copper, brass, and bronze articles may be classed as sacrificial vessels, water-pots, cooking utensils, eating and drinking utensils, other household articles, musical instruments, ornaments for personal adornment and miscellaneous articles. The following is a list of the principal articles made, the names of places mentioned being those of which the articles have been examined:—

## I.—SACRIFICIAL VESSELS.

**Koshá.**—Made of copper, chiefly at Calcutta, Bánsberiá, Navadwip, Dáinhát, and Sántipur. It is an open water-vessel, probably an adaptation of the prehistoric scooped-out rhinoceros-horn. It now resembles in shape the long petal of the plantain flower, and is used to hold water during worship. There are two kinds, heavy and light. Heavy *Koshás* are called *Aghya*, and lighter ones are known as *Májá*.

**Kushi.**—A miniature of above. Used as a spoon to take out water from the *Koshá*.

**Támrakunda.**—Made of copper in the above places. A circular basin with a high rim, in which the idol is placed while being bathed.

**Tát.**—A copper plate on which the idol is placed after washed and while being worshipped.

**Pushpapátra.**—A large copper plate ornamented with flower and foliage patterns. Made in the above places. Used to hold flowers and other offerings intended for worship.

**Paoli.**—A copper water-vessel like the *Lotá*, also called *Ghati*. Made chiefly at Navadwip.

**Ghará.**—A large copper water-vessel used for storing water for sacrificial purposes. Made chiefly at Calcutta. Up-country people also employ it for domestic purposes, but in Bengal *Gharás* for household use are always made of brass.

**Panchapátra.**—A tumbler-like copper water-vessel, with foliage patterns scratched outside. This utensil is mostly imported from Benares. A tiny little spoon accompanies it.

**Kamandalu.**—A prehistoric water-jug, with a handle and a spout. In shape it is a copy of the gourd-shell so often mentioned. It is made either of pure copper or brass, or half of it of copper and the other half of brass. Chiefly imported from Benares.

**Sankh.**—A copy of the conch-shell in copper. Made in Calcutta and other places. Used as an accessory of worship, but not for blowing.

**Báti.**—Cup made of copper, used for holding offerings. Smaller cups, called *Chandan-báti*, are made to hold sandal-paste. Copper cups, called *Katorás* are used by Muhammadans for domestic purposes. Hindus use those made of brass and bronze.

**Sinhásan.**—Throne for idols, made of brass, sides perforated and ornamented with figures of birds, etc. Chiefly imported from Benares. *Sinhásan* as the name implies, is really a "lion-seat"—*i.e.*, a throne supported by a lion This kind of *Sinhásan*, consisting of a lion supporting a lotus, on which the god is placed, is made at Sántipur.

**Garurásan.**—Or the "eagle-throne." Garura, the heavenly bird, is the vehicle of Vishnu. He is represented as a man with wings, the beak of a bird, and clasped hands, supporting a lotus, on which the copper plate, called *Tát*, is placed, with the god in it, when worshipped. Made of brass at Sántipur.

**Padmásan.**—Or the "lotus-seat." A stand with a lotus on the top. Used as above. Made of brass at Sántipur.

**Brishásan.**—Or the "bull-seat." A bull supporting a lotus. Used as above. Made of brass at Sóutipur.

**Chhepáyá.**—An open circular frame supported by six legs, which are decorated in the middle by a single flower and the lower part by a conventional figure of the peacock. Used to hold the copper plate, called *Tát*, with the idol, when worshipped. Made of brass at Sántipur.

**Tepáyá.**—A frame like the above, supported by three legs.

**Tripadi.**—A triangular frame, on three legs, upon which the conch-shell is placed during worship. Made of brass at Sántipur.

**Gilás.**—A brass tumbler, the outer surface decorated with foliage patterns. Used to hold water during worship. Chiefly imported from Benares. *Gilás* is the same as the English word "glass," the European tumbler having been universally adopted for drinking purposes, but instead of being made of glass it is generally made of bronze and to some extent of brass.

**Sáji.**—Flower-basket, imitation in brass of that made of sliced bamboo. Sides perforated, and the handle has a cup on each side for sandal-paste. Used to gather flowers for worship. Chiefly imported from Benares.

**Pancha-pradip.**—Figure of a fairy holding five small lamps in a line. Lit and waved before the idol at the evening ceremony, called *Arati*. Made of brass at Sántipur.

**Ekdip.**—A small single lamp. Used as above. Made of brass at Sántipur

**Dhunachi.**—Incense-burner. Imitation in brass of that made of clay. Used to burn the resin of the Sál tree, called *Dhuna*, during worship and other occasions. Made in Calcutta and other places.

**Karpar-dáni.**—Camphor-burner. A small cup with a long horizontal handle. Used to burn camphor during worship. Made of brass.

**Ghantá**—Bell, with a handle, which is either plain or topped with the figure of the man-bird *Garura*, or by two *Munis* or holy men sitting under the expanded hood of a snake. Made at Sántipur both of brass and bronze. Used for ringing in order to attract the attention of the idol when worshipped. Bells for hanging round the necks of bullocks have a ring instead of a handle.

**Kánsar.**—A gong with a high rim on the back side. Made of pure *Kánsá* or bronze on which the black colour the metal received from the fire in the course of manufacture is left intact, except near the edge, where a broad ring is scraped out all round as an ornamental contrast, and also in the middle, where patterns are formed in the same way. Used for beating during worship in order to attract the attention of the idol, or during an eclipse with the object of scaring away the demons that threaten to devour the sun or the moon, as the case may be. Cuttack has a reputation for this article.

**Ghari.**—A plain solid gong with no rim. Made of bright and pure bronze. Used as above and also to strike the hours. Made at Calcutta.

## II.—WATER-POTS.

**Jálá.**—A large water-vessel, being a modern imitation in brass of the same made in clay. The price precludes its extensive use. Made in Calcutta.

**Ghará.**—A water-vessel made of brass in extensive use. It is also an imitation of the clay utensil, but very old, as gold vessels of this kind have been mentioned in ancient books when wealth and splendour are described. *Ghará* is made both of cast brass and hammered sheet brass. *Dhálá*, or cast brass, has only one join in the middle. That made of sheet brass has two joins, one in the middle and one in the neck. Cast *Ghárás* mostly come into Calcutta from East Bengal, specially Rájnagar in the Faridpur District. Beaten *Ghárás* are made in Calcutta, at Bánsberia, and in the Burdwan District. A kind of *Ghará*, called *Mete-ghará*, a close imitation of the clay utensil, is made at Navadwip. *Ghárás* of a new pattern are made at Budhpárá in Burdwan.

**Kenre.**—A modern imitation in brass of a vessel of this name generally made of clay. It is used for keeping milk and oil. Made at Kálighát, near Calcutta.

**Ghati.**—This is the well-known *Lotá* of other parts of India. It is made of various shapes and sizes, each kind having a name of its own. A few such names may be mentioned here, though it is difficult to describe the characteristic features of the patterns by which they are distinguished from other utensils of the same kind:—(1) *Shámsái*, a long brass *Lotá* made at Bali-Dewanganj; (2) *Dhálá-páoli*, a cast brass vessel made at the same place; (3) *Petá-Mathuri*, a beaten brass vessel, originally brought from Muttra in the North-Western Provinces, now made at Navadwip; (4) *Tukni*, an ordinary brass *Lotá* made at Navadwip; (5) *Dhálá-Mirzapur-Rájdahahi*, a cast brass vessel, imported from Mirzapur in the North-Western Provinces; (6) *Akkelsardi*, brass, imported from ditto; (7) *Káshidl*, brass, ditto; (8) *Kandali Ghati*, ditto; (9) *Chddar-ghati*, made of sheet brass at Simla in Calcutta; (10) *Paldár-ghati*, ribbed, made of brass, at Chandrakona, Midnapur District; (11) *Mungeri-ghati*, a *lotá* of extremely good shape, made of *Bha-ran—i.e.*, impure bronze—at Monghyr; (12) *Chiriádár-ghati*, ribbed, made of *Bharan*, brought from the North-Western Provinces; (13) *Hánsgald-ghati—i.e.* "swan-necked" *lotá* made of *Bharan*, brought from ditto; (14) *Sáhebganj-ghati*, a large vessel with two joinings, made of sheet brass at Sáhebganj in East Bengal. (15) *Jagannáth-ghati*, a *lotá* decorated on the outside surface with foliage and other patterns, made of brass and *Bharan* in Midnapur, Balasore, Cuttack, and Puri Districts; (16) *Kásir-ghati*, made of brass, brought from Benares; (17) *Rámchandrapur-ghati*, made of *Bharan*, brought from Rámchandrapur in East Bengal; (18) *Bildi-chambu*, made of both brass and *Bharan*, South Indian pattern; (19) *Chddarer-mathuri*, made of sheet brass at Simla in Calcutta; (20) *Dhálá-chambu*, made of cast brass at Báli. Smaller *Ghatis* are used for drinking purposes.

**Gáru.**—A brass water-vessel with a narrow mouth and a spout. These are of five kinds:—(1) *Nepáli*—probably the pattern was originally brought from Nepal—made at Báli; (2) *Hánsgald*, or "swan-necked," made at ditto; (3) *Jnter*, made at Khánákul; (4) *Kusure*, small-sized, made at Bánsberia; (5) *Párer*, made at ditto.

**Badná.**—A water-vessel like the above, but with a broader mouth, used by Muhammadans. It is generally made of copper, but sometimes of brass.

**Jag.**—Imitation in brass of the European jug.

**Bhingar.**—Imitation in brass of the Persian *Aftaba.*

**Bálti.**—Brass tub, made largely at Kálighát.

## III.—COOKING UTENSILS.

**Degchi.**—A large cooking-pot, made of hammered sheet copper, chiefly in Calcutta; used tinned by Muhammadans for cooking food in feasts when a large number of people require to be fed.

**Hándi.**—A smaller copper vessel. It is also made of sheet brass and is used by Hindus. Rájnagar has a reputation for its brass *Hándis.* Some of the *Hándis* have an iron rod inside the rim to give it strength.

**Tijel.**—A smaller and shallower cooking-pot, made of sheet brass, used for cooking fish, vegetables, and pulses. This and the above vessel are modern imitations in brass of the clay articles of the same kind. . These have not come into extensive use, as food cooked in them is considered heating and injurious to health. Clay pots are, therefore, still in universal use.

**Golkhola.**—A round cooking-vessel, made of brass at Dáinhát.

**Bharankhola** or **Bokno.**—An old cooking-pot, made of brass at Pútra-sáyer and other places.

**Batna** or **Bantloi.**—A cooking-vessel, resembling *Lota*, but with a wider mouth. Chiefly brought from the North-Western Provinces.

**Sará.**—A cover for cooking-pots, an imitation in brass of the clay article of the same name.

**Dháká** and **Dudh-chhánká.**—Milk-cover and milk-strainer, new imitations.

**Kará.**—Frying-pan. This article was at first made of clay which was called *Khuli.* It was subsequently made of iron, large numbers of which are now imported from England. It is also made in brass, but in limited quantities.

**Khuli.**—A brass pan like the above, generally made in clay.

**Khanti.**—A flat brass spoon, used to stir food when being cooked.

**Hátá.**—Spoon. This is chiefly made of iron. Brass spoons are made at Kálighát.

**Dábu.**—Larger brass spoon with a smaller handle, used to distribute food in feasts.

**Chamohe.**—Spoons of European shape, made at Kálighát.

**Gámlá.**—Brass basin. It is both cast and hammered from sheet brass. Made at Simla in Calcutta. One kind of *Gámlá* has received the name of *Elokeshi* in memory of the murdered woman of Tárakeswar.

**Beri,**—Brass tongs, a new imitation of that made of iron. Made at Kálighát.

**Chhántá.**—A perforated flat spoon, used for straining articles of food when being fried in oil or butter.

**Dhuchuni.**—Rice-washer, a long perforated vessel. This is a new imitation in brass of that made of sliced bamboo. Made at Kálighát.

**Kulo.**—Winnower. A modern imitation like the above. Made at Kálighát.

**Chubri.**—Basket. An imitation like the above.

**Cháluni.**—A perforated utensil used for separating the husk from parched rice. An imitation like the above.

**Dálkánrá.**—An imitation in brass of pestle and mortar. Used to clean pulses before cooking.

**Teler-bhánr.**—Oil-pot. An imitation in brass of the clay article of the same name.

**Chongá.**—A hollow brass tube to blow through for kindling fire. An imitation of a similar article made of an entire piece of bamboo.

**Chaki.**—A circular piece of brass on which flour-cakes are flattened before baking. An imitation of that made of wood.

**Belun.**—A brass roller by which flour-cakes are flattened. An imitation of that made of wood. Most of these modern imitations are made at Kálighát and the neighbourhood, where they find a ready sale among the pilgrims.

**Hamám-distá.**—Pestle and mortar made of brass.

## IV.—EATING AND DRINKING UTENSILS.

**Thálá.**—Large plates are called *Thálás* on which boiled rice is eaten. This is made of copper, brass, and bronze. Copper *Thálás* are called *Nagans*, which are used only by Muhammadans, but to a limited extent, as they have no objection to using brass and bronze articles of this kind. Brass *Thálás* are generally made of hammered sheet brass. Bronze *Thálás* are both hammered and cast. The following kinds of brass *Thálás* may be mentioned :—(1) Ordinary large *Thál*, made of sheet brass in Calcutta ; (2) *Chánch*, made at Bánsberia ; (3) *Ságari*, ditto ; (4) *Parát*, plates with a high rim, brought from Mirzapur ; (5) Large *Thál*, ditto ; (6) *Májá beli*, ditto ; (7) *Beli*, made at Bánsberia. The following bronze *Thálás* may be noted :—(1) *Mihi-kánsá*, made at Kharár ; (2) *Gayeswari*, ditto ; (3) *Bagi*, ditto ; (4) *Báleswari*, ditto, an imitation of that made in Balasore and other parts of Orissa ; (5) *Jagar-náthi Thálá*, made at Balasore, Cuttack, Puri, and other places in Orissa ; (6) *Petá-kánchan*, made at Berhampur ; (7) *Dupit-chhola-Bogi*, made at Berhampur, Khánkrá, and other places in the district of Murshidabad ; (8) *Palicari*, made at Bánsberia ; (9) *Bhuvaneswari*, a cast plate, made at Pátrasáyer ; (10) *Dhálá-kánchan*, ditto. Smaller bronze *Thálás* are called *Kánsis*.

**Rekábi.**—Smaller plates and dishes. From the name, which is a Persian word, it appears that this kind of utensil is of Muhammadan origin. It is made of copper, brass, and bronze ; those made of copper being used only by Muhammadans. *Rekábis* are used for eating tiffins, sweets, fruits, etc. Brass *Rekábis*, especially those brought from Benares, are ornamented with patterns : bronze articles are plain. European porcelain dishes and plates have also been copied in brass and bronze.

**Báti.**—Cups. These are of various kinds, and are mostly made of bronze, though some are made of brass ; but to a limited extent. Cups are used for eating vegetables, pea-soup, milk, and other liquid substances, except water, which is drunk in tumblers and smaller *Ghatis*. The following kinds of cups made of brass may be noted :—(1) *Málá-báti*, made at Dáinhát ; (2) *Mihi-báti*, ditto ; (3) *Bokno-báti*, ditto. The following kinds of bronze cups may be mentioned :—(1) *Achká-khánkrái*, made at Chandrakoná, Pátrasáyer, and other places in Midnapur, Bankura, and Burdwan Districts ; (2) *Jiban-tárá*, or the " star of life," made at ditto ; (3) *Chandrakoná*, made at ditto ; (4) *Namundá-khánkrái*, ditto ; (5) *Phul-poshábi*, or the " fashionable flower," ditto ; (6)

*Sarposhdár*, or "cup with cover," ditto; (7) *Talá-palish*, or "bottom-polished," ditto; (8) *Chinpeydlá*, or "china cup," ditto; (9) *Bit-khánkrái*, ditto; (10) *Mansá-piydli*, or cup sacred to the goddess of snakes, ditto; (11) *Dilkhush,* or "heart-pleasing," ditto; (12) *Gayár-báti*, pattern originally received from Gayá; (13) *Elokeshi-báti*, in memory of the woman of the same name; (14) *Khillure-báti*, from Sri-Kshetra, or the "sacred spot," another name of Puri, the abode of Jagannáth, where it is made; (15) *Báleswari*, made in Orissa; (16) *Gadáddár-báti*, made at a place of the same name; (17) *Bániganjer-báti*, made at Rániganj; (18) *Chiridkhánár-báti*, made in many places; (19) *Krishnakánti-báti*, or the "beauty of Krishna," made at Pátrasáyer; (20) *Birakini-báti*, ditto; (21) *Manmohini-báti*, or "mind-charming" cup, ditto; (22) *Chánd-peydlá*, or the "moon-cup," ditto. Cups, called *Katorás*, are also made of copper, which are mostly used by Muhammadans.

**Páoli.**—A smaller drinking-vessel than the *Lolá*. *Páolis* are of many kinds, such as *Mohanpuri*, *Khánkrái*, etc., taking their name from that of the place where they are made. These are mostly made of *Bharan* and bronze.

**Abkhorá.**—A drinking-vessel of a peculiar shape, probably of Muhammadan origin. Generally made of *Bharan* in Burdwan, Bankura, and Midnapur Districts. One pattern of *Abkhorá*, called *Jahánd*, is largely sold in Calcutta.

**Chumki.**—A drinking-vessel like the *Ghati*. This is an old utensil, but going out of fashion since the introduction of European tumbler-shaped drinking-cups. In all these old-fashioned vessels the uppermost edge is turned outwards, rendering it difficult for the drinker to put his lips on the cups. While drinking he must move his head backward, hold the cup with his left hand, raise it a few inches above his mouth, and pour the water down his throat. To drink by applying his lips to the cup was not considered clean in a caste point of view. Hence, utensils were made out of which water could be easily poured. But the caste rule in this respect has had to give way, as tumblers have been found to be a more convenient drinking-vessel.

**Gilás.**—Tumblers of European shape. These have now come into universal use, and are made in all places, of brass, *Bharan*, and bronze. Those made at Khánkrá in Murshidabad are considered best. The following patterns of *Gilás* may be mentioned:—(1) *Chiridkhánd*, a ribbed vessel, made at Midnapur; (2) *Sarposhdár—i.e.*, "with cover"—made at Khánkrá, Pátrasáyer, etc.; (3) *Geri-chong*, made at Chandrakoná, Pátrasáyer, etc.; (4) *Geri-khánkrái*, ditto; (5) *Sej-gilás*, ditto; (6) *Chong*, ditto; (7) *Khánkrái*, made at Khánkrá and other places; (8) *Paldár*, ditto; (9) *Támd-khuro*, made at Chandrakoná, etc.; (10) *Jalsandes*, consisting of three compartments, the uppermost to hold some kind of sweet, the middle water, and the lowest a betel-leaf with spices. It is, in fact, a sort of tiffin-basket; (11) *Petá-khánkrái*, a vessel of the best quality, made at Khánkrá.

**Dábar.**—A vessel to keep entire betel-leaves. Made of brass at Báli.

**Bátá.**—A circular box, with several small cups to hold betel, lime, catechu, and spices, with which betel-leaves are prepared for chewing. This is a very ancient vessel, but somewhat going out of fashion. The following old lullaby to put babies to sleep is still sung in which *Bátá* occurs:—

> "Ghum-páráni mási-pisi ghumer bári jeo,
> Bátá bhore pán dilo gál bhore kheo."
> "O sleep-bringing aunts let us go to Morpheus' hall,
> We will give you Bátá-ful betel, and chew it all."

*Bátá* is made of bronze at Pátrasáyer, Berhampur, and other places. To a small extent *Bátás* are also made of sheet brass.

**Pán-dán.**—A bronze vessel to keep unprepared betel. These are of two kinds, round and almond-shaped, called *Bádámi*. Made at Kálighát.

**Dibe.**—Betel-holder. An oval box in which betel leaves, prepared for chewing with lime, catechu, cardamom, and other spices, are kept and offered. *Dibe* or *Dibiá* are of various kinds:—(1) *Bel-dibe*, round, resembling the *Bel* (*Ægle Marmelos*) fruit in shape; (2) *Chandrakond*; (3) *Pálish-dibe*—i.e., highly polished; (4) *Mukh-dibe* : the upper part consists of a face, one sort *with* the ears and the other *without* them; (5) *Chándi-dibe*; (6) *Kháukrái-dibe*. *Dibes* are made of bronze, chiefly at Khánkrá, Chandrakoná, Pátrasáyer, etc.

**Gurguri** or **Farsi.**—Smoking-bowl. Made both of brass and bronze. Not much used, except by Musalmans: ordinarily the people prefer *Hukkás* made of cocoanut-shell for smoking the tobacco prepared with molasses or jaggery.

**Kolke** or **Chhilam.**—The *Dhuturá*-flower-shaped pipe in which the tobacco and fire are put. This is generally made of clay, but sometimes copper and brass *chhilams* are also made.

**Sarposh for Chhilam.**—*Chhilam*-covers of brass are made at Sasseram, but the industry is on the decline.

**Baithak.**—Brass stand for *Hukká*, or the smoking-bowl made of cocoanut-shell. The *Baithak* ordinarily consists of an open tumbler-shaped vessel on the top, supported by a leg fixed on a plate-base. *Baithaks* are of various kinds:—(1) *Sáp-baithak*, top resting on an expanded snake-hood, made at Sántipur and Ránaghát ;.(2) *Pari-baithak*, top supported by a fairy and snake-hood ; (3) *Tepdyápari-baithak*, with three legs and a fairy; (4) *Chaupdyá-pari-baithak*, with four legs and a fairy ; (5) *Sejwálá-baithak*, resembling in shape a brass lamp; (6) *S-baithak*, the leg is in the shape of letter S; (7) *Pátwálá-baithak*; (8) *Deyál-baithak*; (9) *Bekábwala-baithak* : this is an old pattern.

## V.—OTHER HOUSEHOLD ARTICLES.

**Pilsuj.**—Lamp-stand, on which boat-shaped triangular lamps, called *Pradip*, generally made of clay, are placed. The following kinds of *Pilsuj* may be mentioned :—(1) *Bábu*—i e., "fashionable"; (2) *Chaupdyá*, with four legs ; (3) *Gol*, or round; (4) *Padma-pdyá*, or "lotus-legged"; (5) *Sámádán* ; (6) *Pari-pilsuj*, with the figure of a fairy. *Pilsujs* are made of brass, chiefly at Ránaghát, Midnapur, Chandrakoná, and other places.

**Pradip.**—Boat-shaped lamps, being brass imitations of those made in clay.

**Fatilsuj.**—Brass lamps of peculiar construction, made at Chatra in Hazáribágh District.

**Chilamchi.**—Washing-basins. Made of brass in Calcutta and other places. Sometimes ornamented with patterns.

**Pikdán.**—Spittoons. Made of brass in Calcutta and other places.

**Bákaa.**—Boxes. Made of brass at Kálighát and in Calcutta Also brought from Benares.

## VI.—MUSICAL INSTRUMENTS.

**Kartál.**—Brass or bronze cymbals. Made in Calcutta.

**Khanjani.**—Smaller cymbals. Made of bronze.

**Mandirá.**—A pair of bronze cups, used to measure time in musical performances. Made in Calcutta.

**Kánsi.**—Small gong made of bronze, beat along with native drums, by boys belonging to the lower castes, who are quite ignorant of music. So there is a proverb current in the country to express want of interest on any particular subject :—

" Bhát khái kánsi bájái, ragarer dhár dhári ná."

" I eat rice, beat *kánsi*, and have nothing to do with notes of music."

**Singá.**—The Indian horn. Made of copper.

**Dug-dugi.**—Brass horn-shaped small drum. Used by religious mendicants and monkey-men.

**Ghungur.**—Small round bells, made of bronze, worn by dancing-girls when dancing to produce a jingling sound.

## VII.—ORNAMENTS FOR PERSONAL ADORNMENT.

Formerly brass and bronze ornaments were largely worn by women of all classes in all parts of Bengal. With the increase of prosperity, however, not only these, but also those made of silver (except for the feet), have almost been entirely discarded by the upper classes in East and Central Bengal. Those who cannot afford to have gold ornaments would rather go without any than wear ornaments made of inferior metals. Low-caste women in these parts use to some extent gold-gilt brass ornaments of good workmanship, made in exact imitation of the gold jewellery of the same nature, and Calcutta is the chief seat of manufacture of such articles. Large quantities of such articles are also brought from Bompás in the Burdwan District. Rude heavy brass and bronze ornaments are made by the Thaterás in Behar and are worn by women of all classes. They are also largely in use in Orissa, as well as among the women of the aboriginal tribes in West Bengal.

The following imitation gold or silver gilt brass ornaments are largely sold in Calcutta :—

**Sinthi.**—A chain worn on the middle of the head where the hair is parted.

**Jinjir.**—Chain to tie up the hair.

**Kántá.**—Hair-pins, topped with flowers.

**Chiruni.**—Comb, worn as an ornament.

**Nath.**—Large nose-ring, worn on the left side.

**Nákchhábi.**—Stud, worn on the left side of the nose.

**Mákri.**—Nose-ring either worn on the left side or through the cartilage of the nose.

**Nolok.**—A small ring with a pearl worn through the cartilage of the nose.

**Dhenri.**—A stud worn on the lobe of the ear.

**Mákri.**—Large and small earrings.

**Mách.**—A fish-shaped ornament sometimes attached to the above.

**Páshá.**—A flat circular ornament, worn through the lobe of the ear. A very old ornament, now going out of fashion.

**Jhumká.**—Flower-shaped earrings, made in imitation of the *Abutilon* flower. Now going out of fashion.

**Karnaphul.**—Literally " ear-flower," a flower-shaped ornament worn through the lobe of the ear.

**Kánbálá.**—Earring worn on the upper part of the ear.

**Kán.**—Ornament of the shape and size of the ear itself.

**Birbauli.**—A broad earring with studs. An old ornament.

**Chaudáni.**—A large earring.

**Pipul-pátá.**—An ear ornament resembling in shape the leaf of the *Pipal* tree (*Ficus religiosa*).

**Dul.**—An earring with a coloured-glass pendant. .

**Chámpá.**—An ear ornament resembling the *Chámpá* (*Michelia Champaca*) flower in shape.

**Kantha-málá.**—A necklace made of elongated beads.

**Mohan-málá.**—A necklace made of round beads.

**Pánch-nali.**—Necklace consisting of five strings of beads.

**Sat-nali.**— Ditto of seven strings of ditto.

**Hár.**—Necklaces of various patterns, such as—(1)*Tárá*, or star pattern; (2) *Hele*, or snake pattern; (3) *Kámrángá*, or Bilimbi (*Averrhoa Bilimbi*), fruit pattern; (4) *Dará*, or cable pattern; (5) *Hánsuli*, or twisted pattern; (0) *Got*, or chain pattern.

**Chik.**—Facetted necklace of good workmanship.

**Hánsuli.**—A collar.

**Mardáná.**—Wristlet made of beads.

**Jabdáná.**—Bracelet of beads shaped like barley.

**Churi.**—Bracelets of various patterns.

**Painchi.**—Bracelet of beads. An old ornament.

**Bálá.**—Ordinary bracelets of various patterns.

**Ananta.**—An armlet, consisting of a hoop highly wrought.

**Báju.**—Flat armlet.

**Bánti.**—A old armlet, which has almost entirely gone out of fashion.

**Tágá.**—Plain armlet.

**Tar.**—Used as above; almost out of fashion.

**Kankan.**—Thin bangles, silver gilt.

**Dam-dam.**—A twisted form of thin bangles, silver gilt.

**Labangakali.**—Bracelet of beads shaped like cloves.

**Nárikelphul.**—Bracelet of beads shaped like cocoa-nut flower.

**Hát-máduli.**—Armlet made of amulet-shaped beads.

**Tábij.**—Armlet made of zig-zag pieces of brass.

**Jasham.**—Armlet made of drum-shaped amulets.

**Chandra-hár.**—Waist-chain with a moon-like tablet in the middle.

**Surya-hár.**—Waist-chain, a modified form of above.

**Biche.**—Waist-chain shaped like a centipede.

**Got.**— Ditto different pattern.

**Batphal.**—Waist ornament for children, made of beads shaped like the fruit of *Bat* tree (*Ficus bengalensis*).

**Nimphal.**—Waist ornament for children, shaped like the fruit of the *Nim* tree (*Melia Azadirachta*).

**Bor.**—Waist ornament for children, made of round beads.

**Komorpátá.**—Waist ornament for children, made of zig-zag pieces of brass.

**Bánkmal.**—A curious-shaped ornament worn on the ankles in West Bengal. It has almost gone out of fashion.

**Gol-mal.**—Round anklet, silver gilt.

**Joren-mal.**—Twisted form of above, silver gilt.

**Páinjor.**—Anklet made of chains and pendants, silver gilt.

**Gujri.**—Anklet worn above *Páinjor*, silver gilt.

**Pancham.**—Anklet worn above *Gujri*, silver gilt.

**Benki.**—Anklet for children, silver gilt.

Brass and bronze ornaments made in Behar and West Bengal are heavy, unwieldy masses of metal, with little or no pretension to beauty or refined workmanship. The following are the most common :—

**Tiká.**—Made of brass, worn on the forehead.

**Jhumká.**—Brass earring.

**Báli.**—Ditto.

**Kánphul.**—Earring.

**Nathni.**—Brass nose-ring.

**Jhulni.**—Ditto.

**Hásli.**—Bronze collar worn on the neck.

**Panwá.**—Brass necklace; also made of bronze.

**Báju.**—Flat armlet like that made in Bengal.

**Tabij.**—Armlet like that of Bengal.

**Churi.**—Bangles. A large number of these are worn on the hand, especially by the women of the milkmen caste.

**Kará.**—Plain bracelets and anklets.

**Jasham.**—Armlets made of drum-shaped beads, like that of Bengal.

**Báutá.**—Heavy armlets.

**Anguthi or chhalla.**—Finger and toe rings with glasses.

**Bichiá.**—Chain worn on the toes.'

**Pairi.**—Heavy anklets.

**Niuri.**—Ditto.

**Paijeb.**—Anklets.

The following ornaments are largely made in Orissa and worn by Uriya women :—

**Kápo.**—Ear-tablet, made of bronze.

**Notho.**—Nose-ring, same as *Nath* in Bengal, made of brass.

**Mákri.**—Earring, made of brass.

**Dandiguá.**—Nose-pendant.

**Kháru.**—Bracelet, made of brass and bronze.

**Tára.**—Armlet made of brass.

**Katni.**—Wristlet, made of brass and bronze.

**Gorbálá.**—Anklet, made of brass and bronze.

**Bankia.**—Anklet.

**Mudi.**—Rings for fingers and toes.

## VIII.—MISCELLANEOUS ARTICLES.

Of late years the manufacture of many new articles in brass has commenced in and around Calcutta, to meet the new wants created with the increase of wealth and love of luxury among the people. Of these may be mentioned—Locks, padlocks, hinges, staples, door-rings, chains, bolts, wrench-bolts, picture-frame hooks, punkha-wheels, gas pendants, gas and water fittings, all sorts of handles, fine wire, castors, brass fittings for harness and carriages, boats and ships, such as capstans, indigo-pressing nuts, boiler fittings, chandeliers, fishing-reels, brass mountings for guns, umbrella tubes (which along with the bamboo handles are exported to England, again to be brought back in the completed umbrellas), hat-racks, knobs, cycle fittings, steam-engine fittings, brass seals, badges, ink-pots, pen-racks, scales and weights and scientific balances of great precision, brass cocks, stands and cages for birds, brass railings, wash-hand stands, buttons, syringes, mathematical and survey instruments, scientific apparatus, surgical instruments, etc., etc. The following detailed list of the last three classes of articles has been supplied by Messrs. Dey, Sil & Co., of Calcutta, who are themselves makers and sellers :—

(1) *Scientific Instruments.*—Apparatus add instruments illustrating mechanical laws; hydrostatical instruments and apparatus; apparatus illustrating laws; experiments on heat; static electrical apparatus; voltaic electrical apparatus, such as electric bells, indicators, pushes, etc.; telephones, microphones, galvanometers; resistance-measuring instruments; fittings for arc and incandescent system of electric light; small dynamo electric machines, electro-motors, electric fans, and useful electrical toys; pneumatic apparatus, such as air pumps, condensing and exhausting syringes, rain-gauges, wind vanes, etc.

(2) *Surgical and Medical Instruments.*—Splints of all kinds, brass syringes, stomach pumps, enema syringes, catheters, pewter medical appliances of all kinds, knives and scissors, forceps, speculums.

(3) *Surveying and Mathematical Instruments.*—Amins' compasses, rectilinear compasses, optical squares, plane tables, land-measuring chains, ordinary dividers, parallel rules, rolling parallels.

Among miscellaneous articles may also be included toys, (of which large quantities are also imported from Delhi) brass mirrors, figures of gods, goddesses, men and animals, and models of vegetables and fruits. Toys chiefly consist of miniature utensils which are given to girls to play house-keeping. They are presented specially to infant brides immediately after their marriage by the bridegroom's family. Brass mirrors were formerly made in Midnapur, Orissa, and the jungle tracts of West Bengal, but these have now been almost entirely superseded by cheap looking-glasses imported from Europe. Brass figures and models are mostly made at Kálighát, Gayá, Sabalpur in Mánbhum District, and certain places in Orissa. Of these the following made at Kálighát may be separately mentioned :—

**Gopál.**—Figure of infant Krishna in a crawling posture, with a roll of butter in one hand and an outstretched peacock feather plume on the head. Coloured red and green in parts. Made of brass of various sizes; largely purchased by *Sádhus*, or religious itinerants, for worship. Other pilgrims purchase it as a house ornament.

**Rádhá and Krishna.**—Two separate figures. Made of various sizes, sometimes 20℔ in weight. Coloured as above.

**Káli.**—The black manifestation of the Primordial Energy.

**Durgá.**—The ten-handed manifestation of above.

**Ganesh.**—The god of wisdom and success with the elephant's head.

**Lakshmi.**—The goddess of wealth and good fortune.

**Saraswati.**—The goddess of arts and sciences.

**Kártik.**—The god of war.

**Mangoes.**—Model of the fruit, hollow, used by pilgrims to keep water offered to gods, called *Charanámrita* or the "feet-nectar."

**Principal Seats of Manufacture.**—Calcutta itself with the suburb are an important centre of copper, brass, and bronze manufactures. Mr. E. W. Collins, C.S., who in 1890 prepared a report for Government on "The Existing

Arts and Industries of Bengal," wrote as follows on the principal seats of such manufactures in Bengal :—

"In almost every town there are shops of braziers, but more than one-fourth of the total number of Bengal are found in the Burdwan Division. There are over 1,300 families of brass-workers in the Burdwan District alone, and the chief seats of the industry are Sáhebganj, Bompás, Dáinhát, Dewánganj, Purbasthali, and Kálná. From the Bankura District over one and-a-half lakhs' worth of brass-ware was exported in 1887. Pátrasáyer is the chief seat of the industry. There are a large number of braziers in the Midnapur District, near Ghátál, and Tamluk, and at Balli in the Jáhánábad Sub-division. The export in 1886 was over 13 lakhs. Kharár in Midnapur employs daily 5,000 men, and is famed for its bell-metal (bronze) ware. In the Hooghly District over 500 families are employed—at Bánsberiá and Khámárpára and the neighbourhood. From Nawábganj and English Bazar in Malda, brass-ware to the value of a lakh of rupees is annually exported. In the Presidency Division, the chief seats of industry are Sántipur, Darmodar, Bánaghát, Maherpur, Daulatganj and Meherpur in the Nadia District, and Bazrápur and Kesalpur in Jessore. In each of these towns some fifty or thirty firms are engaged. Khánkrá Bazar near Berhampur is famous for its bell-metal ware, and twenty-five firms are engaged, each employing eight to ten workmen. In Calcutta there are many firms engaged in Kánsáripárá, where Babu Tárak Náth Parámánik has a large work-shop. In Kamarpárá brass hinges, locks, bolts, etc., are cast. From Cuttack and Balasore there is a large export of brass-ware. Balkati in Puri is also a seat of the industry. In the Dacca Division the town of Islampur and Kágmári in the Attia Sub-division of the Maimansingh District are best known for their brass-work. Over 300 families are employed, and the yearly outturn is over 2,500 maunds. In Patna it is said that there are about 50 families of braziers, and the yearly outturn is estimated at over a lakh of rupees. In Gya brass-work is carried on in several towns, and the yearly outturn is estimated at R30,000. The elegant brass vessels of Nabinagar are much in demand. The west of the Province draws most of its supplies from Mirzapur and the North-Western Provinces, but there are a few skilful workmen at Sewan in Chaprá and Jhanjharpur in Darbhángá."

The following is a more detailed list of the principal seats of brass and bronze manufactures :—

**Bákarganj.**—*Lotás, Gharás,* and other utensils are made here.

**Balasore.**—Brass tubs, *Lotás,* plates, and various other utensils. An oil-bottle of brass and zinc mixed is also made here, which is used for dropping oil on torches during marriage processions, dancing parties, and similar occasions. Another speciality of Balasore is an octagonal betel-dish on four legs. The sale, however, of this particular form of the article is limited, as the price is high and only the rich can afford to purchase it.

**Báli-Dewanganj.**—Burdwan District. Noted for its brass and bronze manufactures, which are largely exported to Calcutta. All kinds of vessels are made in this place.

**Bálkáti.**—Puri District. *Lotás* and plates are made here in large quantities.

**Balli.**—Midnapur District. All kinds of brass and bronze vessels made.

**Báluchar.**—Murshidabad District. Bronze cups, plates, etc., made here.

**Bankura.**—Ordinary bronze cups are largely made here. A *Lotá* with a spout is a speciality of this town.

**Bánsberia.**—Hooghly District. A place noted for its brass and bronze manufactures. All sorts of articles, chiefly of sheet brass, are made here.

**Bázrápur.**—Jessore District. About thirty firms are engaged in the manufacture of brass and bronze ware.

**Begunkola.**—Near Cutwa. Cast tumblers of *Bharan* are made here in large quantities, as well as *Lotás,* cups for sandal-paste, betel-holders called *Dábars,* and brass lamps.

**Belur.**—Howrah District. Large *pikdánis,* spittoons, are made here.

**Berhampur.**—Murshidabad District. Noted for its bronze manufactures. The very best bronze utensils, such as plates, cups, drinking-glasses, are made here and in the neighbourhood. They are justly sought after for their high polish, and command much higher prices than articles of the same kind made in other places. These articles are generally known as utensils of Khánkrá or Khágrá, a place in the neighbourhood of Berhampur.

**Bhadrak.**—Balasore District, and other places in Orissa. Gongs, bells, musical instruments, and household utensils are exported to Calcutta.

**Bishnupur.**—Baukura District. Cups, plates, tumblers, etc., are made here.

**Bompás.**—Burdwan District. Ordinary vessels of brass and bronze are largely made here, as well as gun-metal cups and ornaments, which are sent to Calcutta to be gilded. There are about 200 braziers at work here, who annually produce goods valued at R43,000.

**Budhpárá.**—Cast-brass vessels, such as *Ghardé, Khulis,* etc., are made here.

**Calcutta.**—A quarter of the town, called Simla or Kánsáripárá, contains a large number of braziers. The clang of hammering copper and brass, chiefly the former, can be heard here at all times of the day. Kánsáripárá is also the place where the richest man of this caste in modern days, the late Túrak Náth Paramánik, lived, but he was noted not so much for his wealth nor his extensive transactions in the manufacture and sale of brass and copper ware as for his charity and benevolence. Simla is noted for its copper-ware both for sacrificial use of the Hindus and the domestic use of the Muhammadans. Large quantities of sheet-brass articles are also made here.

**Chandrakoná.**—Midnapur District. A place noted for its brass and bronze manufactures, which are largely exported to Calcutta. Cups, plates and various articles are made here. They are manufactured by people of different castes.

**Chatra.**—Hazaribagh District. *Fatilewj,* or big lamps are made here. These lamps are of peculiar construction and are thus described :—"They consist of three parts. The first part with its plate-base serves as a stand for the other two, and is connected with the second by means of a screw. The third part, resembling a peacock, fits into the socket on the upper portion of the second part. There are also two wings to the lamp fastened on the top of the first part. Common lamp-oil is poured into the receptacles for the wicks and also through the hollow stand of the peacock. When the oil in the burning part is exhausted, an immediate supply is received from the peacock to the hole in its breast, and only in such a quantity as to keep the light burning. This is caused by the air passing through the vacuum between the edge of the peacock's hollow stand and the surface of the remaining oil just after consumption. This process is carried on spontaneously till the oil in the peacock is completely exhausted."

**Chilmári.**—Rangpur District. Various kinds of brass and bronze-ware made here, specially nests of cups.

**Dáinhát.**—Burdwan District. A place noted for its brass manufactures. All kinds of sacrificial vessels and household utensils are made here and exported to other parts of the country. It is noted for its bronze plates and large cooking-vessels. It has 300 families of braziers at work.

**Darmodar.**—Nadia District. Ordinary kinds of brass and bronze vessels made here.

**Daudnagar.**—Gya District. Metal wares are generally made here of the following:—(1) *Pital*, or brass; (2) lead and brass mixed, locally called *Kánsá;* (3) brass mixed with copper, called *Bharat :* (4) pewter, copper, and silver mixed, called *Phulkánsá.* About 200 families of Kaserás and 50 families of Thatherás, with an average of four men in each family, are engaged in the manufacture of metal-ware.

**Daulatganj.**—Nadia District. About 30 firms are engaged in the manufacture of brass-ware. Famous for its small cups.

**Dewanganj.**—Generally coupled with Báli, another place in the neighbourhood, and both famous for their brass and bronze manufactures, which are exported in large quantities to Calcutta.

**Dhaniákháli.**—Hooghly District. Mostly articles of sheet brass are made here.

**Dignagar.**—Burdwan District. Cups, tumblers, etc., are made here.

**Dogáchi.**—Nadia District. *Hukká* stands, called *Baithaks,* with figures of fairies, etc., are made here.

**English Bázár.**—Maldah District. Plates, cups, etc., are made in this place.

**Gadáddi.**—Good bronze cups are made here, which are largely exported to Calcutta.

**Gya Town.**—Sacrificial vessels and other utensils and figures of gods made here. Large numbers of pilgrims flock to this place from all parts of the country, among whom these articles find a ready sale. A kind of brass sacrificial water-vessel (*Panchpátri*) inlaid with copper is made here. Chased copper plates are also largely made which the pilgrims carry away as a memento of their visit to the sacred place.

**Ghátál.**—Midnapur District. Ordinary vessels are made here, specially the water-vessel called *Gáru.*

**Hát-Basantpúr.**—Brass utensils of various kinds are made here.

**Islampur.**—Maimansingh District. Bowls, water-pots, plates, nests of tea-cups, and copper oval spice-holder (*Pán-bátás*), are made in this place.

**Jabui.**—Burdwan District. *Dhuchuni,* or rice-washer, water-pots, etc., are made. The place is noted for its *Gárus.*

**Janganj.**—Balasore District. Cups, plates, betel-holders, etc., are made here.

**Jangipur.**—Murshidabad District. Brass utensils of various kinds are made here.

**Jhanjharpur.**—Darbhanga District. Ordinary utensils are made here.

**Kágmári.**—Maimansingh District. Ditto.

**Kalágeche.**—Midnapur district. Mostly cast brass-ware is made here, such as *Gharás, Páolis,* etc., as well as plates of bronze.

**Káliganj.**—Cups and water-vessels, called *Gárus,* are made here which are exported to Calcutta.

**Kálighát.**—In the suburbs of Calcutta. There is a temple here dedicated to the goddess Káli, a form of the Primordial Energy. Large numbers of pilgrims come here all the year round, who go back to their homes with utensils of various kinds. Articles which were hitherto made of basket-work, wood or clay, are now made in brass, and Kálighát and the neighbourhood is the principal seat of such manufactures. Figures of gods and goddesses in brass are also made here. These articles find a ready sale among the pilgrims. A large number of Kánsáris live at Bhawanipur near Kálighát, but they are now mostly engaged in the manufacture of gold jewellery, silver plate, and surgical instruments.

**Kalna.**—Burdwan District. All kinds of vessels are made. Kalna is also the name of a sub-division, containing several places where brass-wares are largely made. The annual production is estimated at 15,540 maunds, valued at R4,30,839.

**Kánchannagar.**—Burdwan District. A place noted for its brass and bronze manufactures, which are largely exported to Calcutta. Plates, cups, tumblers, and various other articles are made.

**Kesabpur.**—Jessore District. About thirty families are engaged in the manufacture of brass-ware.

**Khanyán.**—Hooghly District. Various kinds of sheet brass and bronze utensils are made here.

**Khámárpárá.**—Hooghly District. Ordinary vessels, brass hinges, locks, bolts, etc., are cast here.

**Khágrábázár** or **Khánkrá.**—Murshidabad District. Noted for its bronze vessels, which are the finest in Bengal and exported to all parts of the country. There are about 25 firms engaged in the work, each employing eight to ten workmen.

**Kharár.**—A place near Chandrakoná in the Midnapur District. Noted for its brass and bronze manufactures, which are largely exported to Calcutta. Capitalists supply the materials and get the vessels manufactured by hand labour, which is cheaper here than in the neighbourhood of Calcutta. Utensils worth about one and-a-half lakh of rupees are annually manufactured at Kharár and exported to Calcutta. The local demand is also considerable.

**Khirpái.**—Midnapur District. Various kinds of *Bharan* and bronze utensils are made here.

**Krishnagar.**—Nadia District. Water-vessels, called *Gárus*, are made here.

**Mahespur.**—Nadia District. About thirty firms are engaged in the manufacture of brass-ware.

**Meherpur.**—Ditto ditto.

**Monghyr.**—Good *Lotás* and other articles are made here.

**Mutiári.**—Burdwan District. Bronze vessels and cooking-pots are largely made here.

**Nabinnagar.**—Gya District. About fifty families of metal-workers reside in this place. The articles are exported to Chutia Nagpur and other places.

**Najumganj.**—Balasore District. Betel-trays and various other articles are made here.

**Nátágarh.**—Twenty-four Parganas District. Brass *Lotás* and other utensils and locks and padlocks made here. There is a colony of locksmiths in this village. Mr. Collins, who visited the place in 1890, made the following notes in his diary :—" There are fifty families of locksmiths at work, and one factory under Babu Dwárká Náth Karmokár, who has ten men under him. They make English padlocks and keys for sale in Calcutta. The brass pieces are cast in the Sukhpur village, where are five brass-casters. They are finished up in his shop and fitted with keys. The work is very neat and the lock complex." Brass locks are also made at Cossipur in Calcutta.

**Navadwip.**—Nadia District. Copper sacrificial vessels, bronze bells, brass *Lotás*, spoons, cups, etc., are made.

**Nawabganj.**—Maldah District. Plates, cups, *Ghárás*, and brass betel-holders are largely made here.

**Patna.**—Ordinary vessels. About fifty families are engaged in the work, and the yearly outturn of utensils is estimated at over a lakh of rupees.

**Pátra-sáyer.**—Bankura District. Noted for its brass manufactures. All kinds of vessels are made here.

**Purbasthali.**—Burdwan District. Cups, betel-holders, and other bronze articles are largely made. The place has 200 families of braziers, who annually produce R30,000 worth of goods.

**Rádhánagar.**—Midnapur District. Various kinds of *Bharan* and bronze utensils are made here.

**Rájnagar.**—Faridpur District. Water-pots, called *Ghárás*, are made here. These are exported to Calcutta.

**Rámjibanpur.**—Bankura District. Cast-brass cooking-pots are made here.

**Ránághát.**—Nadia District.—*Hukká*-stands on snakes and fairies are largely made, as well as images of gods and figures of animals.

**Rániganj.**—Burdwan District. Cups are made here, which are exported to Calcutta.

**Remna.**—Balasore District. Lamp-stands (*Pilsuj*). These lamp-stands are of peculiar construction, not like those commonly found in the country. They have a peacock-shaped oil-reservoir on the top, with a small hole opposite the vessel in which the wick and the oil are kept, and a large square hole below the legs which is fitted in the end of one of the four mouths of the oil-vessel.

**Sabhaganj.**—Midnapur District. Various kinds of bronze utensils are made here.

**Sabalpur.**—Manbhum District. Sacrificial vessels, figures of gods and goddesses, animals, such as horse, deer, fish, etc., and fruits and vegetables.

**Salempur.**—Gya District. Figures of gods and goddesses are made here.

**Sántipur.**—Nadia District. Noted for its brass manufactures, which are largely exported to Calcutta. Sacrificial vessels, *Hukká*-stands, and small figures are chiefly made here.

**Sasseram.**—Shahabad District. Cover for smoking-bowl (*Chhilam*). There are six Kasera families engaged in this work. Some years ago it was reported that the industry was declining, and there was only one man who could manufacture a superior quality of this article.

**Sewan.**—Sáran District. Brass and bronze tumblers. A kind of brass-ware called *Bedhá* is made here. It is of copper and zinc, and made into *Hukká*-stands and other articles. It takes a brilliant polish and is largely sold.

**Sháhganj.**—Hooghly District. There are about fifty Kánsári families in this place who are engaged in making articles of sheet brass.

**Sonpur.**—Cuttack District. Figures of gods and goddesses are made here. One peculiarity of these figures is that they are made of a mixture of copper and brass, but both metals appear separately and distinctly in the same figure. Brass mirrors, called *Suryakánti Darpan*, are also made here. If the face of the mirror be exposed to the sun, and a half-burnt wick of cotton or fibre held opposite to it at a distance of 8 inches, it produces fire. Besides, it has the power of reflecting objects.

**Táki.**—Twenty-four Parganas District. *Hukká* bowls and other articles are made here.

**Tamluk.**—Midnapur District. Ordinary vessels are made here.

**Improvement in Brass-work.**—Mr. E. W. Collins who was deputed by Government in 1890 to report on the existing manufactures of Bengal and to make suggestions for their improvement, made the following remarks on this subject:—

"In addition to what I have said on the subject of designs, the following suggestions are made for the improvement of the various existing industries. Of these, brass work is the most flourishing. It has not yet suffered from foreign competition or the use of machinery. Existing processes, however, are costly, and a great saving of hand labour might be effected by machinery. In spite of the opposition of the braziers, experiments have been made in this direction. The use of dies for stamping the goods to the required shape is, I am told, being, introduced by a European firm in Calcutta. Mr. Biprodas Pal Chowdhari, of Moheshgunge, Nuddea, has made the experiment with fair success. This will save the necessity for hammering out the metal. A few dies and a small hydraulic press are not expensive, and there are many wealthy firms of native braziers who, it they could get over their conservatism, could afford to purchase them. It is doubtful if it would pay to polish and file brass articles with a steam-lathe, as it works too fast, but better hand lathes could be introduced, as has been done by Prem Chand Mistri in his cutlery works at Kánchannagar. The use of imported brass sheets has largely superseded the old plan of making up the alloy in the shops. Punching machines would cause a saving in cutting out the required shape, or the sheets might be rolled into circular pieces in the first instance. I do not think that anything need be taught as to the making of alloys. Native braziers fully understand this business, and the localities where superior brass and bell-metal is cast are well known to the purchasers. In moulding, native workmen do not make their moulds in the ground, but make a separate mould for each casting. If they knew of the system of plate moulding, they would save much time in simple castings. The only place where I saw samples of this work was at the Kánchrápará workshops. The general plan is to prepare a fresh mould on each occasion, and wooden patterns are not used. There are plenty of skilled carpenters who could make the models or patterns in wood, and their use would save time and maintain a regularity of work."

**Conclusion.**—The manufacture of copper, brass, and bronze utensils is perhaps the only important industry which has not suffered from foreign competition or machine-made articles. Several attempts were made to turn out such articles by the aid of machinery, but they have not succeeded. The industry all over the country may be said to be a prosperous one. Almost every town of note has its braziers to make the articles, and shops where they are sold. Besides, hawkers go about from village to village exchanging, like the lamp-seller in Aladin's story, new vessels for old, or selling bright utensils for cash. Owing to the greater purchasing power placed in the hands of the people by the expansion of the export trade in agricultural produce, every household now possesses more utensils than it did in former times, and a larger assortment of such articles is now presented to the bridegroom on the occasion of every marriage, which the bride's father is bound to do in compliance with ancient custom. The industry is, therefore, a thriving one, and there is no sign of its receiving any kind of check in the immediate future. Although porcelain dishes and cups are gradually coming into fashion and enamelled-iron ware has appeared in the market, the use of such articles is extremely limited and does not seem to have made the slightest impression upon the present prosperous condition of the brass and bronze industry.

TRAILOKYA NATH MUKHARJI.

Govt. of India Central Printing Office,—No. 284 D. R., & A.—20-11-94,—160.—A. McL.